SNOW WHITE
⊢ AND THE SEVEN DWARFS ⊢

HIPPO

Hippo Books
Scholastic Publications Limited
London

Scholastic Publications Ltd, 10 Earlham Street, London WC2H 9LN, UK
Scholastic Inc, 730 Broadway, New York, NY 10003, USA
Scholastic Tab Publications Ltd, 123 Newkirk Road, Richmond Hill, Ontario, L4C 3G5, Canada
Ashton Scholastic Pty Ltd, PO Box 579, Gosford, New South Wales, Australia
Ashton Scholastic Ltd, 165 Marua Road, Panmure, Auckland 6, New Zealand

Text and illustrations, © The Mushroom Writers' & Artists' Workshop Ltd London 1986
Produced by Mushroom Books Ltd, London, for Scholastic Publications Ltd.
This edition © Scholastic Publications Ltd.
First published in the UK 1986.
Typeset by Centra Graphics Ltd, London. Origination FE Burman, London. Printed and bound by Mondadori, Italy.

nce upon a time a beautiful young queen sat at a window of her palace, sewing a fine cotton shawl. Outside, snow fell silently. As the queen gazed out, the palace garden soon became covered in a blanket of pure white snow.

The queen, who was not paying much attention to her sewing, accidentally pricked her finger with a needle. Three drops of bright red blood fell on the snow below.

She thought how pretty the red looked against the pure white snow and she said to herself, "Oh, I wish I had a child as white as snow, as red as blood and as black as the wood of this window frame."

Not many months passed before the queen did indeed have a child, a little daughter, who had skin as white as snow, cheeks as red as blood and hair as black as ebony. And so she was called Snow White. But soon after the baby was born, the young queen died.

When Snow White was one year old the king married again. The new queen was a beautiful woman, but she was also proud and vain. In her possession was a magic mirror. Each day she would ask it,

"Mirror, mirror, on the wall,
Who is the fairest one of all?"

And each day, the mirror answered, "You, queen, are the fairest one of all."

As the years went by, Snow White began to grow into a beautiful girl. Her hair was long and thick, her skin was the purest white and her cheeks were rosy red. And because she was kind and gentle by nature, as well as fair of face, she was even lovelier than the proud queen herself.

One morning when the queen asked her mirror,

"Mirror, mirror, on the wall,
Who is the fairest one of all?"

the mirror replied,

"You, queen, both fair and beautiful are,
But Snow White is lovelier by far."

When the queen heard the mirror's answer she became wild with jealousy. From that day on, she sat alone in her room growing more and more envious. Every day she questioned the mirror and each day the mirror would reply,

"You, queen, both fair and beautiful are,
But Snow White is lovelier by far."

Eventually the queen could bear it no longer. She summoned a royal hunstman to her chamber, and ordered him to take Snow White deep into the forest and kill her.

"When you have killed her, bring back her heart to me."

The huntsman trembled at the wicked queen's command, but he had to obey. The king had died the winter before and the queen ruled in his place; her word was law. The huntsman went down to the palace garden where Snow White was playing. He grabbed her roughly and marched her off to the stables. Then off he rode in to the forest.

At last the huntsman stopped. He climbed down from his horse and pulled out his knife. Snow White fell to her knees and begged for mercy. Eventually the hunstman took pity on the young girl and let her go free.

Just then a young boar ran past and after a short chase the huntsman plunged his knife into its side and killed it. He took out its heart and set off back to the palace.

The queen smiled with delight when the huntsman handed her a casket containing the heart. She clasped it to her. For the first time since her life had been overshadowed by Snow White's beauty, the queen felt satisfied.

Snow White, left alone in the forest, was overjoyed to be set free by the hunstman. But as the sun went down she began to tremble with fear. She walked down one dark path after another. Every twig she trod on, every leaf she touched seemed to crackle and echo.

Snow White began to run, faster and faster through the darkening forest. She heard the howl of wolves and the bark of foxes. Black bats flitted on silent wings against clear patches of open sky.

At last, when it seemed she could go on no longer, she came to a little dell and there she saw a small, neat cottage. Crying with relief, Snow White knocked as hard as she could on the front door. There was silence. She knocked again - harder - but there was no reply. Her fear of the forest made her brave and, turning the door handle, she went in.

The little cottage was crowded but tidy. There was a table in the middle of the room laid for dinner. When Snow White came closer, she saw that no less than seven places were laid, but that everything on the table was very small. By each small plate there was a little knife, fork and spoon, and a tiny goblet to drink from. Snow White thought perhaps seven little children lived in the cottage. Surely they would not mind if she had just a taste of their food. She took some potatoes and bread from each plate and from each goblet she sipped a little wine, so that no one would notice anything was missing.

After she had eaten, Snow White felt so tired, she climbed up the little staircase hoping to find a bed in which she could rest. Upstairs she found not one, but seven small beds side by side.

Outside, in the dusk, could be heard the sound of feet marching along the forest path. The owners of the cottage, who were seven dwarfs not seven children, were returning home from work. They worked in a mine, deep in the nearby mountains from dawn to dusk. They carefully wiped their boots on the mat outside and crowded into their little home.

At once the dwarfs realized that someone had been into the cottage because nothing was in its right place. They looked all around but they could see no sign of anyone downstairs. They all crept upstairs and there, on one of the beds, they saw Snow White lying asleep. The dwarfs gazed at the beautiful girl, not daring to move in case they disturbed her. Leaving her to sleep on in peace, they made do with six beds that night. The seventh dwarf slept with each of his companions, one hour with each through the night.

In the morning Snow White woke up and jumped with fright when she saw the dwarfs. But they were friendly and quickly made her feel safe. The seven little men listened quietly while she explained how she came to be in the forest. As soon as they heard her story they said that Snow White was welcome to stay with them in return for cooking and keeping the cottage spick and span.

"You are very kind. I shall be happy to look after your little house," said Snow White.

And so Snow White began a new life as housekeeper to the seven dwarfs. Each morning they would get up early and go off to the mountains in search of copper and gold, and every evening they would return home tired and hungry to enjoy a tasty supper prepared by Snow White. Throughout the day, Snow White was quite alone, with only the forest animals - the squirrels, birds and rabbits - for company. Sometimes a passing traveller would stop at the cottage for a drink of water, or to sell his wares. But each day the dwarfs warned Snow White to be on her guard against her evil stepmother.

The wicked queen, meanwhile, was quite sure that Snow White was dead and that, once again, she was the most beautiful woman in the world. But after a while she wanted to hear the mirror tell her so. Dressed in her finest robes, she went to her mirror and demanded,

"Mirror, mirror, on the wall,
Who is the fairest one of all?"

and the mirror answered,

"You, queen, both fair and lovely are,
But over the hills, in the greenwood dell,
Where the seven dwarfs do work and dwell,
Snow White is safely hidden, and she
Is fairer far, O queen, to see."
The queen was horrified. She knew the mirror never lied. The hunstman had deceived

her and Snow White was still alive. Day and night she thought of how she might kill her stepdaughter until at last she was ready with a plan.

Disguised in a shabby cloak with her face stained so that she looked like an old pedlar, the queen trudged over the seven mountains to the forest where the seven dwarfs lived.

When she came to the cottage she called out, "Pretty things to buy," and held out some brightly coloured laces. "This one would suit you," she said.

The sight of the pretty laces was too much for Snow White she opened the door wide and invited the old woman to come inside. As soon as the queen was inside the cottage she seized her chance. "Let me lace you properly," she said, "and you will look so pretty." Snow White eagerly agreed.

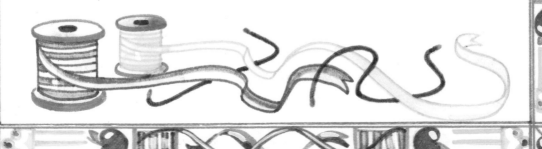

The queen took the laces that the girl had chosen and quickly and deftly laced her bodice for her. Snow White gasped, the laces were so tight. She went cold with fear when she saw the look of triumph on the old woman's face.

It was too late. The laces had been pulled so tight that Snow White could not breathe. She fell to the floor as if she were dead.

Gazing down at Snow White lying there quite still, the queen muttered, "Now I am the fairest in the land!" And she hurried away in triumph.

It was not long before the dwarfs returned home from their day's work, thoroughly tired out. Snow White was not in her usual place by the cottage window, nor did she come to the door to welcome them.

Anxiously the dwarfs opened the front door and to their dismay saw Snow White lying slumped on the floor. They rushed to lift her up and seeing that her bodice was laced far too tightly, they at once cut the laces.

The dwarfs watched Snow White for the faintest flicker of life. At last they saw her take a deep breath. Soon she opened her eyes and sat up. When she told them what had happened they immediately guessed that the old pedlar was really the wicked queen in disguise. Shaking their heads sadly, they warned her again not to trust any strangers or let anybody into the cottage.

As soon as the queen reached home she rushed to her mirror, longing to hear again that she was the fairest in the land.

She asked,

"Mirror, mirror, on the wall,
Who is the fairest one of all?"

The mirror replied as before,

"You, queen, both fair and lovely are,
But over the hills in the greenwood dell,
Where the seven dwarfs do work and dwell,
Snow White is safely hidden, and she
Is fairer far, O queen, to see."

"It's a mistake!" shrieked the queen. But knowing the mirror never lied, she set about making new plans to put an end to Snow White.

The queen was also a skilful witch, and with the help of her powers she made a beautiful but poisoned comb. Once again she disguised herself but this time as a different old woman, shrivelled and bent almost double. The following morning she set off on the long journey to the dwarfs' home. At last she came in sight of the pretty little cottage in the dell.

The queen rapped loudly on the door. Snow White gasped and then called out, "Who is it, please?"

"It's only a poor old woman hoping to sell a few combs and trinkets, my dear. Come and look at my pretty goods."

Snow White felt tempted, but remembering the dwarf's warning she called out, "I cannot let anyone in."

But the queen was cunning, and with her clever talk she overcame Snow White's fears.

"There's no need to open the door," she said. "Just look at my combs through the window."

Snow White ran to the window and leant out. The combs were difficult to resist.

"This would look lovely in your hair," said the old woman holding the comb against Snow White's hair.

"Do you really think so?" asked Snow White innocently.

This was all the encouragement the old woman needed. Leaning forward, she quickly pushed the comb into Snow White's hair. Hardly had she done so than the poison started working and Snow White fell down unconscious.

"You're done for now," said the queen. And with that, she turned to go home.

When dusk fell, the seven dwarfs came home. When they found Snow White lying on the floor they were sure her scheming stepmother had managed to harm her again. They soon found the new comb in Snow White's hair and took it out. Scarcely had they taken it out when Snow White stirred and opened her eyes.

When she told the dwarfs what had happened, they warned her once more to be very careful and never to let anyone in or buy anything from a stranger.

When the queen reached home she went at once to her mirror, and demanded,

"Mirror, mirror on the wall,
Who is the fairest one of all?"

The mirror answered as it had before,

"You, queen, are fair and lovely too,
But over the hills in the greenwood dell,
Where the seven dwarfs do work and dwell,
Snow White is safely hidden, and she
Is fairer far, O queen, to see."

Then the queen felt angrier than she ever had before. "Snow White shall die," she shrieked, "even if it costs me my life."

The queen hurried to the most secret room in the palace, high up in the round tower. As she entered, she was greeted by a black crow.

"I have important work to do," she muttered.

The crow cawed back to the queen.

"Poison apples, you say? Do we have anything deadly I can put into a tempting apple to poison Snow White?"

The crow raised a tattered wing and seemed to point with his beak to the far side of the room. There flasks of murky liquids bubbled. The crow's beady eyes shone bright with excitement as the queen distilled a vicious potion.

At last she held up the results of her work - a shiny apple, red on one side and yellow on the other, so cunningly made that only the red side was poisoned. Then, disguising herself as an old farmer's wife, the queen set out towards the forest again.

It was morning by the time the queen reached the home of the seven dwarfs. She approached the door, walking slowly and limping slightly, her basket of apples over her arm. She knocked at the door…rat-tat tat-tat.

From inside Snow White called out, "Who are you and what do you want?"

The wicked queen answered in a quavering voice, "Let me rest here for a while. My poor feet are so sore."

Snow White looked out of the window and said, "I am not allowed to let anyone in."

"Well then, I'll just pause to get my breath back, if you don't mind. I'm too old to go traipsing around day and night to earn a few pennies."

Snow White at once felt sorry for the tired old woman and ran to fetch her some water. The old woman leaned on the windowsill, making it seem as if she was panting for breath.

"Thank you," she said when she had finished the drink that Snow White handed her. "Here, have an apple, dear. I'll give you one, although they sell fast enough for good money."

"No," said Snow White, "I dare not take anything."

"Well, you won't be poisoned if that's what you're afraid of," cackled the old woman. "Look, I'll share this one with you." She held out a big shiny apple, yellow on one side and rosy red on the other. "You have the red part and I'll eat the yellow."

Snow White looked at the basket of glossy fruit and smelled their delicious sweet fragrance. The woman cut the apple in half and began to eat the yellow part. Snow White watched longingly. The apple looked so sweet and juicy - and surely there could be no danger, for the old woman was eating it herself. She stretched out her hand to take the other half of the apple. The old woman watched eagerly as Snow White put the red apple to her lips, and hardly had she taken one bite before she fell down, quite dead. That evening when the dwarfs returned home that is how they found her.

Meanwhile the queen had cast off her disguise and hurried home to the palace.

When she had dressed herself in all her finery and was satisfied that she was looking her best, she went to her magic mirror. Now she would find out the truth. Had she really managed to kill Snow White? Was she rid of the girl for good?

She asked the mirror,

"Mirror, mirror, on the wall,
Who is the fairest one of all?"

And this time the mirror answered, "You, queen, are the fairest one of all."

Then, at last, her jealous heart was satisfied. Her beautiful stepdaughter was well and truly dead.

Frantically the dwarfs had searched around for the cause of Snow White's death. When they found the poisoned piece of the apple lying by her head, they knew at once that this was the queen's evil work.

Lifting up Snow White they tried every way they could to revive her, but it was useless, she was dead.

Throughout the night the grief-stricken dwarfs sat up keeping watch over the body of their beloved Snow White. But by morning they realized that there was no longer any hope. They laid her upon a bier and sat round it for three days, weeping bitter tears.

Snow White looked so beautiful as she lay there with her rosy red cheeks and her ebony hair, that they could not bear to bury her in the dark ground. Instead, they made her a glass coffin, so that she could be seen from every side, and they laid her in it.

They scattered fresh flowers inside the coffin and on the side, in gold letters, they wrote her name. Then the dwarfs placed the coffin on the mountainside and took turns to watch over it.

The word soon spread over the mountains and through the forest that Snow White was dead and, one by one, all the birds and animals of the forest gathered by the side of the coffin to mourn the girl who had been so kind and gentle. First came an owl, then a raven and last a dove; so, too, came the rabbits, the deer and the squirrels whom Snow White had befriended.

For a long time Snow White lay in the glass coffin on the mountainside. But her beauty did not fade with each passing day. Through all this time, she looked just as if she were asleep.

Now one day a prince strayed into the forest by mistake. He was the only son of the king of a neighbouring land, and while out hunting he had become separated from his companions. He had ridden through the forest all day, and his horse was tired and in need of water.

As night fell, the prince rode into the clearing where the dwarfs' cottage stood. Knocking at the door, he asked for a night's shelter. The dwarfs gladly invited him to come in.

As he talked with the little men, the prince asked them if they knew anything about a glass case with a beautiful girl lying inside?

The seven dwarfs sighed sadly. They told the prince about Snow White and how they had sheltered her. They explained that she had lived happily with them until her wicked stepmother had found out where she was and how, in the end, she had succeeded in killing Snow White.

They talked late into the night. Before they went to bed, the prince vowed that he would see Snow White in her coffin before he left the following day.

Early the next morning the prince said goodbye to the dwarfs and, true to his word, rode to the hillside where he might see Snow White.

Gazing down at the beautiful girl, the prince felt his heart ache with longing. Never had he loved anything in his life as much as he loved Snow White. Leaping on his horse, he galloped back to the dwarfs' cottage and asked them to give him the coffin. In exchange he would give them whatever they asked.

But the dwarfs said no. "We would not part with it for all the gold on earth," they said.

"Then give it to me as a gift," pleaded the prince, "for now I have seen Snow White, I cannot live without her. I will honour and treasure her all my life."

He spoke so sincerely that the dwarfs were moved to pity and though it nearly broke their hearts to do so, they at last said that he could have the coffin.

SNOW WHITE

Joyfully the prince rode back to his father's kingdom. He gathered together his servants to ride back with him to the forest, to bring Snow White's coffin back to his own land.

The prince ordered his servants to take the greatest care so as not to jerk or jar Snow White. But one servant stumbled over the root of a tree and, as he did so, jolted the coffin. At once, the poisoned piece of apple that Snow White had bitten off came out of her mouth. Then she began to breathe, slowly at first and then more quickly. After they had gone a little farther, Snow White opened her eyes, lifted the lid of her coffin and sat up.

"Heavens, where am I?" she cried in amazement.

The prince hardly dared to believe that his deepest wish had come true. But it *was* true - Snow White had come back to life. Clasping her small hands in his he told her everything that had happened since she bit the evil apple, and as she gazed at him and listened to his voice, Snow White fell in love.

"Please be my wife," said the prince.

Snow White blushed modestly but her own heart was beating fast as she whispered agreement.

And so the young couple rode on to the prince's land, and there announced their engagement.

There was joy throughout the land at the forthcoming wedding between the prince and Snow White, and preparations were soon taking place. The streets were decorated with flowers and flags, the palace lined with velvet carpet. The seamstress worked day and night to sew a wedding gown for the bride from the finest cloth of gold.

One day, an invitation to the wedding feast of the young prince and his new bride arrived at the palace of Snow White's wicked stepmother.

Delighted at the prospect of showing off her beauty before such a large crowd, the queen spent days choosing her most flattering robe and best jewels for the occasion.

When finally she was ready to set out for the wedding feast, the queen went to her mirror to be reassured of her supreme beauty. She asked, as she always did,

"Mirror, mirror, on the wall,
Who is the fairest one of all?"

and the mirror answered truthfully,

"You, queen, both fair and lovely are,
But the new made bride is fairer far."

When she heard the mirror's reply, the queen howled with rage and jealousy. She had taken so much time to get rid of Snow White and now another rival had appeared in the shape of this new bride! Her rage was so great and her envy so huge that her life was made completely miserable. Her pride told her to ignore the invitation, but jealousy made her want to see the young bride and compare her beauty with her own.

At last the wicked queen decided to attend the feast just to satisfy her burning curiosity. So she journeyed to the neighbouring kingdom and arrived when the wedding feast was in full swing.

Boldly the wicked queen strode up to the throne where the newly-wed couple sat, so that she could look more closely at the bride. As soon as she recognized Snow White in a cloth of gold dress, her face turned red with fury and she began to scream with rage. The sound was terrible to hear. Then suddenly she collapsed, shaking to the floor. A doctor was called but he was too late. The queen was stone dead. The shock of seeing Snow White alive had proved too much for her wicked heart.

Now that her evil stepmother had met with the punishment she so thoroughly deserved, Snow White no longer lived in fear for her life. Loved by the seven dwarfs, who had come to live in a little cottage in the palace grounds, by all her subjects , and most of all by her husband, Snow White lived in peace and great happiness for the rest of her long life.